DTT 221378

HOW TO BUY A CAR

DANIEL COHEN

PHOTOGRAPHS BY
MAUREEN McNICHOLAS

FRANKLIN WATTS
New York • London • Toronto • Sydney • 1982
A TRIUMPH BOOK

Our thanks to the following for
their help in photographing this book:
Mr. Dennis Mahaffey, Dave Badinger,
Crystal Bass, Joel Hughes,
Blake Locklin, Edith Hellman,
Trina Lloyd, and Gary Velasco.

R. L. 2.9 Spache Revised Formula

Library of Congress Cataloging in Publication Data

Cohen, Daniel.
How to buy a car.

(A Triumph book)
Includes index.
Summary: Discusses the expense involved in buying and
maintaining a car; whether to choose a new or used car;
and how to select, buy, pay for, and insure an automobile.
1. Automobiles—Purchasing—Juvenile literature.
[1. Automobiles—Purchasing.   2. Consumer education]
I. McNicholas, Maureen, ill.   II. Title.
TL162.C63   629.2′222   82-6899
ISBN 0-531-04494-7   AACR2

CONTENTS

HOW TO BUY
A CAR

1

SO YOU WANT TO OWN A CAR

Almost everybody wants a car. Cars get you where you want to go when you want to go. You don't have to depend on others. No more begging for rides. No more missing out because you can't get there.

Cars are great. But they are also a big pain. Before you go out and buy a car, ask yourself two questions: Do I need a car? Can I afford one?

If you don't have to worry about money you can skip the rest of this chapter. If you are like most of us, and you do have to worry, read on.

What do you need a car for? Do you need it to get to work or school? Are there other ways of getting where you must go? In many cities public transportation is much faster and cheaper than private cars.

Can you get rides from your friends or co-workers? Does your family own a car that you can borrow when you need one? Sure, it would be fun to have your own car. But would it really be worth all the expense and trouble?

You have probably thought about all of this already. And you figure you still need that car. OK. Go on to the next question. Can you afford it?

That's the hardest question. Money is the biggest problem in owning a car. Cars cost lots of money. The prices of cars are going up all the time. And the price that you pay to buy the car is just the beginning. If you have to buy a car on time there are the finance charges. They are going up all the time too.

Even if someone gives you a car free, it's going to cost you money. There are registration fees and insurance. Insurance alone can cost you hundreds of dollars a year.

Just keeping a car running is expensive. Gas costs a lot. It is probably going to cost more. It certainly is not going to cost less. In Europe people pay $2 or $3 a gallon for gas. You may be paying the same one of these days.

No car runs perfectly forever. Cars break down and must be fixed. Repairs cost money. If you buy an old car because it is cheaper, it will probably break down more often. That will cost more. Even if you can fix the car yourself, parts are not cheap. And you probably won't be able to fix everything yourself. Cars need oil changes, tune-ups, new tires, and other regular maintenance. All of this costs money.

Do you have a safe place to park your car? In many cities overnight parking places are hard to find. Sometimes, cars parked on the street are broken into. Or they are stolen. In some areas you may have to pay to park.

At one time it seemed that practically everybody could afford a car. Cars were a part of the great American dream. Driving around was a favorite pastime. That's not true anymore. Times have changed. People are buying fewer cars and driving them less.

Do you know what kind of car you *really* want? Of course you do. So do I. Well, forget that one! You can't afford it and neither can I.

Let's be practical. Will you get a new car? Or is a used car best for you?

BUYING A NEW CAR

10,000

If you can afford $6,000 or more, you can start thinking about a new car. That's what the *cheap* ones cost. Price is the big problem. New cars are usually much more expensive than used cars.

But if you can handle the big up-front cost there are lots of advantages. In the long run a new car may even cost you less. It should also be less trouble. In

The car of your dreams may not
be the practical choice.

most cases, a new car will run better and last longer than a used one.

⚡ The new car dealer will give you a warranty. That means the dealer agrees to fix things that go wrong within a certain period of time. These repairs are free. Usually warranties are for twelve months or 12,000 miles (19,200 km), whichever comes first.

A warranty doesn't cover everything. If you get a flat tire or smash up the car, the dealer won't fix that for free. Some warranties don't cover items like windshield wipers or light bulbs. Others do. You will have to check. The differences between new car warranties are usually minor.

No warranty is perfect. If you get a real lemon, a warranty may not help much. The car can spend more time in the shop than out. Some dealers will loan you a car free while your car is being fixed. Others will not. You could find yourself without any car. Sometimes, the dealer may not be able to fix what is wrong.

If you get a lemon you won't get your money back. And the dealer won't give you another new car. One auto company has offered a "money back" guarantee with a thirty-day or 1,000-mile

(1,600-km) limit. But that's only one company. And that guarantee is very limited.

Some people who bought lemons have sued the dealers. Usually they don't win. Even when they do, it takes a lot of time and trouble. In most cases, you have to keep bringing the car back until they fix it correctly. And sometimes they never do. Buying any car is a bit of a risk.

Luckily, the total lemon is rare. In most cases, the car runs as it is supposed to. Or the dealer can fix it.

That brings up another advantage of a new car. The dealer has, or should have, the parts to fix what is wrong. With used cars you can never be sure. Parts can be expensive and hard to get.

So, a new car should save time and money on repairs. It will probably also save on gas. American driving habits have changed over the past few years. Once, people drove big cars. The cars had eight-

All new cars come with a warranty.

VEHICLE LIMITED WARRANTY

...rrants all parts (except those referred to below) of ...TSUN vehicle supplied by NISSAN to be free from ...terials or workmanship under normal use, service ...ce for 12,500 miles or 12 months, whichever ...om the date of delivery to the original retail ...e date the vehicle was first put into service, ...r.

...ARRANTIES, INCLUDING WARRANTIES
...BILITY AND FITNESS FOR A PARTIC-
...HALL BE LIMITED IN DURATION TO
...TIME AND THE MILEAGE SET FORTH
...ALL NOT BE RESPONSIBLE FOR INCI-
...QUENTIAL DAMAGES, SUCH AS LOSS
...EHICLE, INCONVENIENCE OR COM-
...E STATES DO NOT ALLOW LIMITA-
...Y AN IMPLIED WARRANTY LASTS
...OR LIMITATION OF INCIDENTAL
...AMAGES, SO THE ABOVE LIMITA-

TIONS OR EXCLUSION MAY NOT APPLY TO YOU. THIS WARRANTY GIVES YOU SPECIFIC LEGAL RIGHTS, AND YOU MAY ALSO HAVE OTHER RIGHTS WHICH VARY FROM STATE TO STATE. THIS IS THE ONLY EXPRESS WARRANTY APPLICABLE TO *DATSUN* VEHICLES. NISSAN NEITHER ASSUMES NOR AUTHORIZES ANYONE TO ASSUME FOR IT ANY OTHER EXPRESS WARRANTY.

NISSAN will, at its option, repair or replace with a new or re-manufactured part any part covered by this warranty which becomes defective, malfunctions or otherwise fails to conform with this warranty under normal use and service during the term of this warranty at no charge for parts or labor. In order to obtain warranty repairs, the vehicle must be delivered to an Authorized *DATSUN* Dealer in the United States or Canada at the owner's expense. The names and addresses of Authorized *DATSUN* Dealers are listed in telephone directories or may be obtained by writing or telephoning any of the offices listed inside this booklet.

This warranty does not cover:

1. Tires and tubes and emission control system parts. These

1

OWNER'S MANUAL

cylinder engines. It didn't matter if they only got 10 or 12 miles (16 or 19 km) to the gallon of gas. Gas was cheap.

But gas isn't cheap anymore. The smaller the car the less gas it uses. Four-cylinder cars usually use less gas than six-cylinder cars. Eight-cylinder cars are less popular. Most American cars now get 25 or 30 miles (40 or 48 km) per gallon on highways. And the mileage is being improved every year. With the price of gas today, that's something to think about.

Size is a good guide to judging the gas mileage of a particular model. But size isn't the only thing that counts. All new cars have estimated mileage ratings posted. These ratings are made by the government. They are not perfect. The average driver will not get as many miles per gallon as the ratings indicate. But they are a starting point. Check them carefully. Gas mileage may not mean much to you at first. It will mean more every time you stop and say, "Fill it up."

Gas mileage isn't the only matter to consider. Smaller cars are sometimes more expensive. This is particularly true of the sporty two-door models.

You have to decide what size car you need. Very small cars can be cramped. If you are tall or big, driving a small car can be uncomfortable. If you expect to carry a lot of passengers, a small-sized car can be a big problem.

What options do you want? Automatic transmissions make driving easier. Manual transmissions save gas.

With a new car you can order just the style and color you want. And it can be ordered with as many or as few options as you want.

Ordering a car, rather than picking it off the lot, takes time. It may be weeks or months before your new car is delivered. You don't have a chance to test drive it before you pick it up. But if you are particular, and can wait, it might be worth it. Dealers are stocking fewer and fewer cars. So, you are less likely to find what you want sitting in the showroom.

You're not going to own your car forever. One day you will want to trade it in. The newer the car the higher the trade-in value.

A new car is a huge investment. It's probably the biggest investment you have ever made. Don't get carried away just because you like the looks of a car. Don't be taken in by some slick ad. Check it out.

Do you know anybody who owns the kind of car you're interested in? Talk to them. Find out what they think is good about the car. And find out what they think is wrong with it.

Do you know any mechanics? If you do, talk to them too. Find out what they think of different cars.

There are lots of magazines that rate new cars. Everything from *Road and Track* to *Consumer Reports*. Find out what the magazines have to say.

In the end, the decision is yours. Just make sure you have all the facts before you decide.

BUYING A USED CAR

Let's say you haven't got the money for a new car. You will have to buy a used car. Sometimes a used car can be a great deal, better than a new car.

You have to be very, very careful when you buy a used car. Here is why. Today, new car prices are so high, more and more people are buying used cars. People are also keeping their cars longer. That means there are fewer used cars to sell, and more people to buy them. Many used cars have had a long, hard life. They may not be in very good condition. Yet the prices are still pretty high for most used cars. Your best bet is probably a larger car.

Sometimes used cars can cost more than new ones. Take the Edsel. The Edsel was put out by the Ford Motor Company in 1957. It was a big, ugly gas guzzler. It was a disaster. By 1958, people hated it. Very few Edsels were sold. Two years after it was put on the market, the Edsel was dropped. It was considered the biggest goof in auto marketing history. For years, people joked about how terrible the Edsel was.

You might think an Edsel would be worth nothing today. But the Edsel is now rare, so it has status. People pay much more for an Edsel today than they did when the car was new. The car isn't any better. It costs a fortune to fix. But you can't argue with a car collector.

The Edsel isn't the only old car that costs more today than it did when it was first made. Practically any car that is over 25 years old and in good condition can be considered a "classic." The price goes way up on "classic" cars.

If you want a car for driving, not collecting, don't buy a very old car. Don't buy an exotic used foreign car. Avoid "orphans"—models that are no longer in production. Even if the cost is rock bottom, it's a false saving. The cost of parts and repairs will be very high. You may not be able to get the parts. You may not be able to find someone who knows how to repair an old car.

What if your heart is set on a "muscle" car—one with air scoops, racing stripes and extra-wide tires? They show up on used car lots. They tend to be expensive. But sometimes the price on this kind of car is too good to be true. Be careful. The person who owned the sporty model probably drove it hard. Hidden underneath that bright paint, there may be many problems.

Think twice about cars with a lot of power options. Power windows and power seats are not really necessary. They raise the price. Worse still, they often go wrong. Even on new cars they are trouble. On used cars they are worse. And they are expensive to fix.

Every used car is different. But some models hold up better than others. Ask around. Find out what experiences other people have had with different kinds of cars. There are also a number of good books with useful information. One of the best is *Consumer Report's Guide to Used Cars.* It tells you about hundreds of different used car models, both foreign and domestic. It tells you the best bets in used cars, and the worst. You may not agree with *Consumer Reports.* But what they have to say is at least worth hearing. They are not kept in business by auto advertising, so they can tell it straight.

Buying a used car is always a bit of a gamble. But it is a gamble you can win, if you know what you are doing.

3

WHERE SHOULD YOU BUY IT?

NEW CARS

There is only one place to buy a new car. That is at a new-car dealer. But you must pick the right dealer. This is just as important as picking the right car.

Let's say you decide to buy a brand new Xmobile. But the nearest Xmobile dealer is 50 miles (80 km) away. Sure it's easy to get there to buy the car. But you will have to go back regularly to have it serviced. Warranties require that the car be serviced by the dealer. If it isn't, the dealer doesn't have to honor the warranty if something goes wrong. So, you will have to go back to the dealer many times. And you will have to hang around while the car is serviced. You can waste a whole day that way.

Repairs are an even bigger problem. What if your new Xmobile starts making a horrible noise? You must drive it 50 miles (80 km) to the dealer, if the car is still on warranty. If the car just stops, you must have it towed. Towing is usually covered by the warranty, but it's still a problem.

Say you have to leave the car for a day or longer. How are you going to get home? Some dealers will loan you a car. Sometimes, this is even part of the warranty. Don't count on it though. Sometimes, a dealer will arrange to have you driven home. But most of the time you are on your own. You will have to arrange your own transportation. Can you afford to rent a car? And once you are home you have to pick up the car when it's ready. If you are lucky and your new car is relatively trouble-free, fine. The long trip is well worth getting the car you want.

Choosing a good new-car dealer is almost as important as choosing the right car.

But what if you have to go back many times for repairs? Think about it.

You may decide to settle for a Ymobile. There is a Ymobile dealer just a few blocks away. If you can't start the car you can push it to the dealer.

The location of the dealer is one thing to think about. There are other things to consider. A dealer's reputation is important. Does the dealer have a good service department? Does the dealer keep his or her promises? Will he or she stay in business? If a dealer goes out of business before your warranty is up, you may get stuck. Other dealers who handle the same make will honor the warranty. But another dealer may be far away. Sometimes, they will service their own customers first. Customers from other dealers come last.

You have to ask around. Talk to people who have bought cars from different dealers. See what they think.

Then there is the deal itself. How much is a car going to cost you? Car prices for the same model with the same options can vary from dealer to dealer. Shop around if you can. See where you can get the best deal.

In the window of every new car is a list of what the car with its options will cost. That's called the sticker or list price. It's just a starting point. Most cars sell for less than the sticker price. The dealers expect this. If a dealer is overstocked in a particular model he or she may sell well below the sticker price. If the model is popular it may sell at close to or even above the sticker price. Don't forget the local sales taxes. They may not always be listed on the sticker.

The early fall may be a good time to buy a car. The new models are coming in. The dealer wants to get rid of his old models. He or she may be willing to lower the price. Don't expect any half-price sales. But you can save money.

From time to time, auto manufacturers have offered rebates. That means you get money back. You pay for your car. Then the auto manufacturer sends some money back to you. Keep an eye out for rebate deals. If they are around, you won't have to look too hard. When a particular manufacturer is offering rebates there are big signs in the dealer's window. Rebates are usually offered at times when cars are not selling well.

Knowledge is power, when you are buying a

car. The dealer will probably tell you he or she is offering you the rock-bottom price. That may be true. And it may not be true. Try to find out what the dealer had to pay the factory. There are a number of auto price books with this information available at newsstands. Add to this price anywhere from $200 to $500 for dealer's expenses and profits. That will still be hundreds of dollars below the sticker price. Don't expect to get the car for that price, unless it's a model the dealer is trying to unload. It's a price to start with when you bargain.

Don't buy a car you really don't want just because you can save a few hundred dollars. A car is a big investment. You will probably have it for years. So, you should like it. If you can afford it, get what you like or the nearest thing to it.

An important part of buying a new car is picking the options. Options can be anything from bumper guards to air conditioning. Some are useless, some are nice, and some are even necessary. Some are relatively cheap, and others are very expensive. They all raise the price of a car. So carefully figure the costs before you choose the options.

Some dealers sell a special treatment to preserve the finish on the car. This can cost $100 extra or more. An ordinary wax job is just as good. That may cost only $10. Undercoating and extra rust-proofing may not be necessary either. On the other hand, a rear window defogger or defroster is almost a must. Avoid option packages if you can. This is a group of options sold together. The dealer may offer you a special price. But you may not need or want the whole package.

When you walk into the dealer's showroom you may become confused. You may be dazzled by all the shiny new autos. Be prepared. Start your shopping at home. Find out all you can about the cars you are going to look at. Have a fairly clear idea of what you want. That way, you can concentrate on getting the best deal. If you don't know what you want, the dealer ends up with the best deal.

USED CARS

There are many places where you can buy a used car. The safest place is probably a new-car dealer. New-car dealers take used cars as trade-ins. Then they try to sell the used cars. New-car dealers usually charge more than other used-car sellers. One reason for this is because they have better used cars. Cars in poor condition are sold to used-car dealers. New-car dealers' main business is new cars. They don't want a lot of old cars cluttering up their lots. They want cars in good condition that will sell quickly.

New-car dealers have their own service departments. They can fix up a car before selling it. Most used cars sold by new-car dealers come with some kind of a warranty. These used car warranties are more limited than a new car warranty. But if something goes wrong, the dealer's shop probably can make the repairs.

The reputation of the seller is very important, especially when buying a used car. Anyone can sell a clunker by accident. But if a dealer regularly sells bad cars, that's no accident. Ask around. Find out as much as you can about a dealer.

Be extra careful when shopping for a used car.

A dealer who specializes in used cars usually has cheaper cars for sale. But watch out! Remember those cars the new-car dealer didn't want to bother with? They wind up on used-car lots.

Used-car dealers also sell a lot of cars from rental agencies, taxi companies, and police departments. Such cars have had a much harder life than ordinary cars. The extra wear and tear might not show up when the car is sitting in the lot. But after you've driven the car a few weeks or months, big problems can develop.

Sometimes, car rental agencies or other owners of large numbers of cars hold special sales. These will be advertised in the newspaper. In these sales, only the best of the used rental cars are sold. The prices tend to be fairly high, but you may get a good buy.

The clunkers from the rental agent, like the clunkers from the new-car dealers, usually wind up on the used-car lot. It's just another reason to be careful when buying from a used-car dealer.

In general, used-car dealers do not have a good reputation. There are plenty of honest dealers—but there are many dishonest ones as well. Dishonest dealers don't usually stay in one place very long. Used-car dealers who have been in the same place for a long time are your best bet. Established dealers have a reputation to uphold. If too many customers complain about them, business will suffer. Then they will have to close up or move somewhere else where they aren't known.

A big drawback to buying from used-car dealers is their lack of service. Used-car dealers often have small service departments. You are less likely to get good service from a small service department. Some used-car dealers don't have service departments at all.

The great advantage of used-car dealers is that they have less expensive cars. So it may be a gamble worth taking. But be very careful, or you could really get stung.

A private sale is yet another way to get a used car. Newspapers are filled with classified ads for used cars. However, a lot of these ads are placed by used-car dealers. Call and check it out first. If the seller turns out to be a dealer and the ad didn't say so, forget it. That's just a come-on. If the dealer tries to fool you with an ad, just think of what he or she will

do with a car. You may also see a car you like with a "for sale" sign on it and the owner's telephone number.

A private sale can be a good deal. In theory, you eliminate the middleman—the dealer. So the car will cost you less, and the seller will make more. You won't get an old taxicab, either.

Private parties can sell some awful cars. But the car's problems are usually obvious. A dishonest dealer may be able to hide a car's defects. Private parties don't often have the skill for that.

As usual, there are disadvantages along with the advantages. You won't get a warranty in a private sale unless the original warranty hasn't run out. There is no service department where you can bring the car for repairs. And there won't be a dealer to handle the paperwork. You'll have to handle it. And you'll probably have to make a quick decision and pay cash on the spot.

A private sale can be a good deal.

You may buy a car from a friend or relative. You know the seller, and probably the history of the car. But there are some pitfalls. Haggling over price can create hard feelings. What if something goes wrong with the car? Perhaps the relative or friend who sold you the car didn't know there was something wrong. But you'll be angry anyway. You can wind up with a lemon and a new enemy. That's no bargain.

How do you know if you are paying a fair price for a used car? Before you buy any car check the "book price," or the *NADA Official Used-Car Guide*. The book is a publication of the National Automobile Dealers' Association (NADA). It isn't sold at newsstands. A bank officer might let you look at a copy. Bank officers use them to check prices when making car loans. An auto dealer might let you look at his or her copy. Some libraries stock the *Official Used-Car Guide*.

The book lists both the wholesale and retail prices. A dealer will probably charge you the full retail price. In a private sale you should pay a figure halfway between the wholesale and retail price.

4

HOW NOT TO GET TAKEN

You have checked your bank account and decided it has to be a used car. Now you are going out to look for one. You think you know something about cars. You know a good deal when you see one. No one can fool you. If that's what you think, you're in for trouble.

A dishonest used-car dealer will outsmart you every time. Even in an honest deal there are many problems you might overlook. Rule number one is: be humble. You don't know it all. Take someone with you, preferably someone who knows a lot about cars. If you're young take someone who is older. Young buyers are often thought of as easy marks.

When you find a car that is of interest, look it over carefully. Ask if you can take it for a test drive. If the dealer won't let you, walk away. Just looking at a car can tell you a lot. But driving a car will tell you much more. The seller who won't let you drive a car may be hiding something. Don't take a chance.

*Here are some used-car buying tips offered by *Consumer Reports*:

• Go shopping on a sunny day. Darkness or rain makes judging a car harder.

• Check the mileage on the car's odometer. That should give you an honest record of the number of miles the car has been driven. There is a federal law against tampering with an odometer. But it's done anyway. So look at the inside of the car. Pay particular attention to the driver's seat. Is it worn and lumpy? Does the driver's windowsill look worn? If so, the car may have had a lot of hard use. If the odometer mileage is low, get suspicious.

• Next, look at the tires. If they are badly worn or brand new and the odometer reads low mileage,

Always test drive a car before you buy it.

get suspicious. How did they get so worn after only a few thousand miles? Or why did the seller have to change them?

• Check for uneven tire wear. That may indicate a host of problems. Some may be serious, some may not.

• Look for rust. Small rust spots are easy to fix. Repairing severe rust is expensive and sometimes impossible. Be sure to check under the doors and in the wheel wells. Those are parts of the car that often rust.

• Examine the surface of the car. It may be rippled here and there. Or the color may be slightly different in places. If that's the case, suspect major body work. The car may have been in a severe accident. There's nothing wrong with that, as long as the car has been fixed properly. But an accident can do more than dent a fender. It can cause serious internal damage that you can't see. Also, the repaired and repainted surface may rust more quickly. Don't reject a car just because it's been in an accident. But be extra careful.

• Open and close all the windows and doors. Do they work properly?

- Grab the top of one of the front tires. Shake it hard. Does it seem loose? Is there a "clunking" sound? That could mean trouble. Check both of the front tires in this way.

- Stand at a corner of the car. Push down hard on the fender or bumper a couple of times. Let it up quickly. The car should stop bouncing. If it doesn't the car probably has bad shock absorbers.

- Crawl under the car. Look at the exhaust system. Is it rusted out? Are there holes in it? Look for dark or damp places on the ground. Oil or transmission fluid might be leaking.

If the car passes this first inspection, take it for a drive.

- Start the car. How does the engine sound? Strange noises could mean expensive trouble.

- Try the lights, the wipers, the defroster, and everything else powered by the car's electrical system.

- Try all the gears, including reverse. Pay attention to the steering. It should "feel" right.

- Drive the car over bumps. How well does it hold the road?

- Find a level stretch of road with no traffic. Try

to find a puddle. Let your friend out of the car. Have him or her watch the wheels as you drive slowly away. The car should move straight, not at an angle. This is easier to see if you can drive through a puddle. The tracks of the rear wheels should follow those of the front wheels exactly. If they don't, the car may have been in a serious accident and may have a damaged frame.

• Test the brakes on the same stretch of road. Get the car up to 45 miles (72 km) per hour, then brake. Of course, you must be sure no one is behind you. Do this three times. The car should stop straight, with no pulling to either side.

• Head for the highway. Drive at highway speed for a while. Take your foot off the accelerator for several seconds. Then step on it hard. Does a cloud of blue or white smoke come out of the tailpipe? That is not a good sign. The engine may need an overhaul.

Check under the hood,
and have a mechanic
look the car over.

Don't expect a used car to be perfect. Especially if it is an inexpensive one. But you don't want to be stuck with a lemon.

If you think the car might be worth buying, there is one more step. You have done all you can. Now it is time to get professional help. This will cost you money, but it's worth it. Tell the seller you want an independent mechanic to take a look at the car. If he or she refuses, you would be wise to walk away. The seller may be trying to hide something.

A mechanic or an electronic diagnostic center will charge you from $25 to $50, possibly more, for an examination. Tell the mechanic about anything strange you noticed during your test drive.

Tell the mechanic to write out what is wrong. And have him estimate the cost of fixing the car. Take the estimate back to the seller. If the car needs a lot of additional repairs, you may be able to get the seller to reduce the price. It's a bargaining point, anyway.

If you follow these suggestions you'll increase your chances of buying a good used car. But there are no guarantees. If you buy the car and then discover serious problems, ask the seller to make repairs. He may refuse. Some used-car dealers will offer a limited warranty or a warranty on certain parts of a car.

What if you think you have been cheated? You can complain to the local department of consumer affairs. Or you can contact the state attorney general. Or you can sue. All of this takes time. In the end you may not gain anything. Buying a used car is always a risk.

5

PAYING FOR
YOUR CAR

By now you have lots of information on different kinds of cars. Your head is swimming with facts to remember. Your clothes are dirty from crawling under cars. Your ears are strained from listening for strange engine noises during test drives. You're wondering about the smiling car dealer. "Is he telling me the truth? Was this car really owned by a little old lady who only drove it to church on Sunday? Why did she need racing stripes and air scoops to go to church?"

You are tired, confused, and maybe even a bit frightened. But you have made a decision. You know what you want. Are your troubles over?

Difficult as it was, picking a car was the easy part. Now comes the hard part. You have to pay for it. How will you do that?

Could you pull out a roll of bills, peel off a few big ones, and hand them to the dealer? If you did, the dealer might faint. Or he might call the cops. He would figure you stole the money. At the very least, he would check the money very carefully to see if it was phony. Cash sales of cars are not very common.

At one time the best way to pay for a car was to take the money out of your savings. This was assuming that you had savings. If you wanted to build up your savings again, you could put money back in every month. In a way, you were borrowing from yourself.

The next best thing to do was have a bank finance the car. The dealer could also arrange to finance a car. That usually cost more. Now, however, inflation and high interest rates have changed the picture.

For example, you may have several thousand dollars. But you may not keep it in a savings account. You may have your money in a savings certificate, a money market fund, or some other investment. These investments pay much higher interest than a savings account. Sometimes, you can't take money out of these investments whenever you want. In other cases, you may not want to. The money you make through your alternate investments may be more than the interest you will pay if you borrow money to buy the car.

Most commercial banks still offer auto loans. But the interest rates are very high. Many savings banks and savings-and-loan associations that once offered car loans now do not.

Since car sales have dropped, car dealers are especially eager to sell their stock. A loan arranged through a dealer is easier to get. It will probably cost more than a loan arranged through a bank. But it may be a much better deal than it was just a few years ago. Dealers will often finance cars for people who can't get bank loans.

The money picture is changing all the time. What might be good advice today could be very bad advice next year—even next month. So when you decide to buy, shop around for credit. It's just like shopping around for anything else. See who has the best deal.

If you have to borrow to buy a car, remember that borrowing money *costs* money. Let's say you

need to borrow $6,000. And let's say that you get the loan at an interest rate of 15 percent a year. That's a pretty good rate at the moment. And let's say that you decide to pay the loan back over four years or forty-eight months. That is average for a new car loan.

By the time you have paid that loan off you will have paid $2,015 in interest. That means the car will really cost you $8,015, not $6,000. You will have to make payments of $167 a month for four years.

An extra $2,015! That's a lot money. Can you pay less interest? Yes, if you pay the loan off more quickly. Pay it off in thirty-six months, or three years, instead of in four. Then your total interest will be $1,488. That represents a saving of $527. But there's a catch. If you decide to pay off your loan in thirty-six months, your monthly payments will be

How will you pay for
your car? First, take
a look at your budget.

$208. That is $41 more every month for thirty-six months.

What if you don't want to pay $208 every month? Even $167 a month takes a big bite. You could stretch out your payments over five years or sixty months. Your monthly payment would be only $143. But by the time you are through paying for the car you will have paid an extra $2,564 in interest. Your $6,000 car will now cost you $8,564!

When you apply for an auto loan, don't just ask what the monthly payments are. Find out how much total interest you will have to pay. That will give you a more accurate idea of the cost of your car.

Most people still get their auto loans from a commercial bank. Naturally, the bank wants to be sure that you will pay back the loan. So, it is best to pick a bank that knows you, and that you know. If you have a checking or savings account at a particular bank, it is the first place you should try. Some banks give lower interest rates to customers who have accounts. Banks will also give lower interest rates to people who have previously borrowed money and paid it back on time.

Usually, you won't get a loan for the full price of

a car. You have to make a down payment. An average down payment is about 25 or 30 percent of the total cost. If your car is going to cost $6,000, you will need to pay at least $1,500 as a down payment. But the amount of the down payment required varies.

The dealer will give you a statement of the cost of the car. Take that to the bank. The bank will then decide whether it will lend you the money. You may have trouble finding a bank that will finance some used cars. If the car is more than four or five years old or if it has a poor resale value, the bank might not want to lend money on it.

When you take out a car loan, the bank really owns the car until you pay off the loan. If you don't pay the loan, the bank takes the car. The bank then sells the car to make its money back. Old clunkers are hard to sell. Banks are not in business to lose money. So, they don't usually finance old cars.

If you are buying your first car, you probably have not borrowed a lot of money before. You don't have what banks call a "credit record." That could be a problem. Banks don't like to lend money to people who have a bad credit record or no credit record.

That may seem unfair. You can't borrow money unless you have a good credit record. And you can't get a good credit record unless you borrow money. It *is* unfair—but that's how it is.

All is not lost. A new borrower can get a loan with a comaker, or cosigner. This is a person who already has a credit record. He or she also signs for the loan. If you don't pay it back, the cosigner is responsible.

When you apply for an auto loan at a bank you will be given an application to complete. The bank wants to know how you will pay back the loan. Most of the questions on the application will be about how much money you make. The bank wants to know how long you have worked at a particular place. And it wants to know how long you have lived at a particular place. If you have stayed in one place for a long time, that's good. The bank assumes you won't run off with the car.

The bank will also want to know about your other expenses. Do you pay rent? If so, how much? Do you owe money? If so, how much? It's best to tell the truth. If you owe a lot of money to a store and don't report it on your loan application, the bank will find out. Most businesses belong to central credit bureaus. These businesses report who owes how much. Any financial institution, such as a bank, can look at these records. If you're not telling the truth, you probably won't get the loan you want.

Some credit bureaus have very complete records. These records may contain personal information. Have you or anyone in your family ever been arrested? That information could be in the records. Information supplied by your neighbors could also be in the records. Many people don't think that credit bureaus should keep such information. But they do.

If you are turned down for a loan, ask why. In most parts of the country, there are laws that require banks and other places that lend money to give the reasons. Perhaps, there are mistakes in your credit record. If there are, try to have it corrected.

At times, there is plenty of money around. Banks are then less strict about making loans. At other times, money is tight. Loans are harder to get. Larger down payments may be asked for. There is no way of predicting what the loan situation will be when you want a loan.

If you intend to borrow from a bank, talk to a bank officer before you look for a car. Find out if you can get a loan at all. Get an idea of how much you will be able to borrow. You may find you will have to wait a few months until the credit situation eases.

Paying for a car is a serious business. If you don't make your payments on time, you will be hit with a late charge. That will be 10 or 20 percent more on every payment more than two weeks late. A couple of late payments won't cause any problems. But if you are almost always late with your payments, the bank or other lender won't forget. Late payments will go on your credit record. The next time you try to borrow money, you may not get what you need.

What if you don't pay at all for several months? The bank will go to your cosigner to collect. The cosigner was probably someone who liked and trusted you. That friendship and trust will be shattered.

If you don't have a cosigner or the cosigner won't pay, then the lender can take the car. You will be left with a very bad credit record, no car, and nothing to show for the payments you did make. You will be a big loser.

There are a couple of other places that sometimes make auto loans. If you are a member of a
credit union, that is a good place to start. Credit
unions sometimes make auto loans. Credit union
interest rates are usually reasonable. Private finance
companies also make auto loans. They will lend money to people who can't get a bank loan. Sometimes,
they will lend money to people who can't get dealer
financing. Finance companies' interest rates are
much higher than the rates charged by banks or
most dealers. If you have to go to a finance company to get your car, you probably shouldn't be buying
one.

Finally, you can borrow from a relative or friend.
You may not have to pay any interest at all. And the
lender won't be so strict about making payments on
time. But there is a risk here, too. If you don't pay or
if you pay very slowly, there can be hard feelings.

6

CAR
INSURANCE

You have picked out your car. You have had your loan approved. And you're ready to drive off, happily ever after, right? Wrong!

There is one more big hurdle to overcome— insurance. You need insurance. And this insurance will probably cost you several hundred dollars a year. Why do you have to get insurance? Because most states have laws that require some form of insurance. You are not allowed to own a car unless you have insurance. But there is a good reason for these laws.

Let's say you are driving along and you hit another car. You wreck it. Never mind your own car for the moment. Could you afford to pay the other driver for his car? Or worse, what if someone in the other car was badly hurt? Could you afford to pay the hospital bills? Probably not.

Turn the problem around. What if someone hits you, wrecks your car, and puts you in the hospital. Don't you think the other driver should pay? What happens to you if he or she can't pay?

Most people simply can't afford to pay the expenses in a major accident. That's why the law usually requires some kind of insurance. This is called liability insurance.

There is another kind of insurance. Say you park your car on the street for the night. When you come out the next morning, you find someone has hit it. You don't know who did it. But there is a lot of damage. You can be insured against this. Or say you are driving along and a dog runs in front of your car. You swerve to avoid hitting the dog. You miss the dog but hit a telephone pole. There is insurance that will cover that as well.

Liability insurance
is a must.

If your car is stolen or broken into, your insurance can cover it. If a tree limb falls on your car or your car catches fire, insurance will cover that. However, insurance will not pay for normal wear and tear on a car.

Auto insurance is a complicated subject. What you need and the cost will vary from state to state. Sometimes it varies from neighborhood to neighborhood! The requirements are different for different cars and for different drivers. To find out how much insurance you will need and how much it will cost, talk to someone who sells auto insurance.

Insurance costs plenty. This is particularly true if you are a new driver and if you are young. You will have to pay much more than an older, more experienced driver for the same coverage.

Perhaps this is unfair. But here's why it is done. Insurance companies set the cost of their policies— or premiums—by statistics. According to statistics young, inexperienced drivers have more accidents than older, more experienced drivers. The insurance companies have to pay out more. So they charge more.

Maybe you feel that you have better reflexes and eyesight than older drivers. That may be true. But it won't lower your premiums one cent.

After you have driven for a couple of years and if you have no accidents, your premiums may be lowered. However, the cost of insurance has risen steadily. So, it is more likely that your premiums just won't go up as fast.

If you have a couple of accidents, the insurance company will pay for the damages. But your premiums will go up—and fast. If you have many accidents, the insurance company may cancel your coverage. In most states, the law says you must have insurance. You can't drive your car without it. If you are caught driving an uninsured car, you are in big trouble. You can be fined. You can even go to jail. Don't try it.

Your insurance can also be canceled if you don't pay on time. So pay your premiums when they are due.

If you live in a city your premiums will probably be higher than if you live in the country. There are more cars in the city. There are more chances of an accident. And more cars are stolen. The insurance company's risk is higher. So, you are charged more.

Most states require that you carry insurance to cover the other driver's losses in an accident. Insurance to cover your losses is optional—unless you have borrowed the money for the car. Banks require you to carry insurance to cover the cost of the car. This is because they actually own the car. They don't want to take a loss. If your car is totally destroyed the bank gets its money back from the insurance. The more expensive the car and the higher the coverage, the higher the premiums will be. It costs more to insure a $10,000 car than it does to insure a $5,000 car.

So, in most cases you don't have much choice about insurance. The state and the lender tell you what you must have. But if you have an older car that's all paid for, you do have some choice. You can reduce the amount of coverage on your car. That will lower your premiums. If it's a very old car, you may want to cut out all insurance on it. That doesn't mean liability insurance—only the insurance on your own car. It may be worth risking a total loss on the car and saving the extra premiums you would have to pay. But remember, today even old cars are expensive. So, think hard before dropping your coverage.

There are lots of companies that sell auto insurance. And there are many different ways of selling insurance. Some companies even sell auto insurance through department stores.

The premiums vary, even for the same coverage. The service also varies. Some companies pay claims quickly and efficiently. Others are slow and give you a hard time.

Your best bet may be to find a good local insurance agent. Most agents sell insurance from a number of different companies. A good agent will find you the best deal. The agent will also explain what you *must* have, and what you *should* have. And the agent will handle all the paperwork. If you are in an accident, you will file your claim through the agent. The best agent is someone you trust, and someone who is nearby.

How do you find a good insurance agent? There are no rules. The best thing you can do is find out who your friends and neighbors recommend.

7
THE FINAL STEPS

By now you may have shelled out thousands of dollars for a car. And you have agreed to pay hundreds of dollars for insurance. Don't put away your checkbook quite yet. You still have to pay registration fees. They average from $10 to $30. That may sound like peanuts after what you have already spent. But it is against the law to drive an unregistered car. If you do, you can wind up in court.

Every state has different fees. Every state has a different set of regulations for registering your car and getting plates for it. And every state requires you to have a different set of papers to prove you own the car.

If you're buying from a dealer, you don't have to worry about any of this. The dealer will take care of it all. Of course, you'll have to pay the fees.

If you buy a car in one state, but live in another, that can cause some confusion. You will probably have to reregister the car in your home state. Talk to the dealer. Explain the problem. You may also have to go to the motor vehicle department in your home state. If you know you're going to buy out of state, find out what is involved before you buy.

Sometimes a dishonest dealer will sell an unregistered car. Such cars are usually stolen. This doesn't happen often. But it does happen. If you suspect that there is something wrong with the registration on the car you are buying, call off the deal. No matter how good the deal may look, you are buying nothing but trouble.

If you are buying your car from a private individual, you may have to take care of the registration yourself. Check with the nearest motor vehicle office. Find out what the law requires. Find out what papers you are supposed to get to prove you legally own the car.

In most states, the seller should give you a signed document called a Certificate of Title. This certificate is then taken to the proper government agency and registered. A new Certificate of Title is then issued to you.

Most states require some sort of inspection of a car every year. A few states require an inspection twice a year. In states that do require inspection, you can't register a car unless it has been inspected. Find out when your car's next inspection is due. And have the car inspected on time. It will cost only a few dollars. Inspections are done by government agencies or licensed service stations. If you don't get your inspection, you can get an expensive fine.

Regular inspections are a good idea. They are usually very simple. They won't tell you if your car is running well. They will only tell you if it is safe. Inspectors check the tires, brakes, and lights. In some states a check is made of auto emissions. Is the car polluting the atmosphere? If your car can't pass a basic safety inspection, it shouldn't be on the road until it is fixed.

If you are thinking of buying an old car, or one that is in poor condition, remember those inspections. The car you buy may run. But if it can't pass inspection, you won't be allowed to drive it. And repairs may be expensive.

All new cars come with an owner's manual. It's a little book that tells you how the car works. It also tells you about regular maintenance. It shows you how to start your car on a cold morning and the most common reasons why your car won't start. The owner's manual contains lots of interesting and important facts about the model of your car. If you have a new car, look the owner's manual over carefully before you do a lot of driving.

Most car owners leave the manual in their glove compartment. Often, it is still there when the car is sold. So, if you buy a used car, look for the owner's manual. It should come in handy.

By now you have done all the looking. You have talked to all the people. You have signed all the papers. You have paid all the money. And the car is finally yours. Now, you can start thinking about selling it!

There are two schools of thought about owning cars. One person may buy a car and drive it for a certain number of years. Then he or she trades the car in on a new or used car.

Another car owner may have a different idea. This owner may buy a car and then drive it as long as possible. When the car is literally falling apart, the owner will then try to trade it in or sell it. A car that is falling apart won't bring much. Sometimes, it can be sold only for junk.

Which car owner is smarter? There is no clear answer to that question. Both approaches have good and bad points.

The older a car gets, the more it has to be repaired. After you have had a car for a few years, expect repair costs to go up.

But cars are very expensive. And if you have to finance one at high interest rates, that is even more expensive. The payments on a new car will probably be much higher than the repairs on your old one. Most of the time, it costs less money to keep a car running as long as possible.

At some point, you may decide to have a major overhaul job done on your car. You may also decide to have the car completely repainted. All of that can cost hundreds of dollars. But it may be worthwhile. You won't have a new car. You will have a car that runs better and looks better than the one you had been driving. Considering the cost of new cars, that can be a great bargain.

Money isn't the only factor. There is also safety. Older cars aren't as safe as new cars. Even if an old car is kept in good repair, the steering may be loose. The brakes can begin to go. Many things can wear out, making it less safe.

Most old cars are less reliable. If you really depend on your car, that factor can be very important. An old car may not start if it gets too cold. It can stall in the rain. There are lots of reasons why an old car can suddenly stop running. At that point you should start thinking about another car.

And you might just get tired of driving a car you have had for years. You may want something different. Feeling good about a car is important too.

Whether you intend to trade your car soon or drive it forever, it makes sense to take care of it. Every so often give your car a personal inspection. Use some of the suggestions in Chapter 4 for testing a used car. Ask yourself: "Would I buy this car now?" Are your shock absorbers going? Do your brakes seem to be giving way? If you have an oil leak, do something about it. Don't wait for an emergency.

If you don't know a lot about cars, find a good mechanic. Have the car checked regularly. This will help you avoid some costly repairs later on. You may also avoid costly, embarrassing, and sometimes even dangerous breakdowns on the road.

It's no fun to have your car stop on a busy

highway. You may have to be towed away. A ride in a tow truck is one of the most expensive rides you can take.

The most common minor emergency is a flat tire. If you don't know how to change a tire, learn. All cars should carry a jack and a spare tire. Many of the newer cars have only temporary-use spare tires. These are good enough to get you to the nearest service station. But you can't take any long drives on them. It is better to have a full-sized spare. You should also carry a tire pressurizing can. Several types are available. If your puncture is small you can use the can to inflate the tire for a short time. You can then drive to a service station. Or you can at least drive to a safer spot in which to change your tire.

Carry a tool kit if you know how to fix cars. If you don't, there are still some items you should keep in your car. A flashlight is a must. Check it every once in a while to see if the batteries are OK. When you do need a flashlight you will want one that works.

A couple of flares are also good. A car that is stopped on a road at night can be dangerous. If you

put out some flares, you will be much safer. So will other drivers.

Thick insulating tape can be very useful. You can use the tape to temporarily seal a split hose. Many drivers also carry an extra fan belt. It is easy to learn how to change a fan belt. For snowy climates a brush and ice scraper should be on hand. For really snowy places many drivers carry a pair of tire chains.

Still another helpful item is a jumper cable, for starting a car with a dead battery. But make sure you know how to use the cable. If you don't, you can get a nasty shock.

At one time you could pull into a gas station and say, "Fill'er up and check the front end." The attendant would put in the gas. Then he or she would open the hood and check the oil, the amount of water in the battery, and the transmission fluid level. The attendant might also look at the water level in the

Learn how to change
a flat tire.

radiator and examine the windshield wiper blades. If you went to a gas station regularly the attendant might remind you when your oil needed changing and when a regular tune-up was due.

That doesn't happen as often anymore. More and more gas stations are "self-service." The gas at these stations is a little cheaper. But you have to check the front end, and everything else yourself. Your owner's manual will tell you what you have to do for your car. If you don't have an owner's manual, or are just not sure of yourself, here is a tip. Go to a full service station for at least one fill-up out of every four. Try to find a station where the attendant has the time to check the oil, water, and other things. The gas may cost a bit more but it's worth it.

A regular oil change is absolutely necessary. You can ruin your engine if you don't change your oil. How often you should change depends on the kind of car you have, the type of oil you use, and the

*Change the oil in
your car regularly.*

conditions under which you drive. Check your owner's manual.

You can change your own oil and oil filters. The job is not a hard one, but it is messy. If you don't know what to do or don't have a place to do it, let the service station do it. It won't cost that much extra. Regular tune-ups can save gas. A lot of people now do their own tune-ups. If you don't know how to tune your car, have it done by an expert. Or have an expert show you what to do. It's not the sort of job you can learn from a book.

If your car has a windshield washer spray, and most cars do, make sure it has plenty of fluid. If your windshield wipers begin to wear out, get new ones. These are the kinds of little things that most drivers put off. Then one day it rains, and they find they can't see. Don't let that happen to you.

Carry a tire pressure gauge. Use it often to test your tire pressure. Properly inflated tires wear longer and save gas.

Keep the outside of your car clean. The car looks nicer. A clean car is more resistant to rust. This is particularly important if you live where it snows a lot. In order to make snow-covered roads less slippery, salt is spread on them. The salt melts the snow. But when it sticks to your car, it dissolves the paint and other surface coating. This opens the way for rust. Rust is the greatest destroyer of car bodies. Washing your car will get rid of the salt. When you wash your car, wash underneath as well as on top. The salt collects under the car.

If you follow all the rules—and with a little luck— you and your car will have a long and happy life together.

INDEX